From the Eye of Africa to the Floating Island of Atlantis in the Sargasso Sea

Vito de la Vera

From the Eye of Africa to the Floating Island of Atlantis in the Sargasso Sea

My Voyages

Counterfactual Archeology

Editor: Institutio de la Vera
Proof reading: Le Club d'Aventure d'Outre-Mer
Front page picture: L'Atelier d'Aventure d'Outre-Mer
Translation: Le Club d'Aventure d'Outre-Mer

Publisher: BoD · Books on Demand GmbH, In de Tarpen 42,
22848 Norderstedt, Germany

Printing: Libri Plureos GmbH, Friedensallee 273, 22763 Hamburg, Germany

ISBN: 978-87-4306-012-3

EYE OF AFRICA, MAURETANIA

We were cruising along on a desert road in Mauritania. L'Aguila had been left moored in the harbor of Nouakchott. I did not often venture this far inland from my beloved yacht that has brought me so far and wide, but the trail had led us here on the road into the Sahara. Angelo was at the steering wheel. Thankfully, as I do not like driving that much.

Our findings had led us here much to my surprise. I had not expected our journey to research some rock carvings on the Canary and Cape Verde islands would lead us ashore and into the Sahara, but it soon became clear that we had stumbled onto something important. Maybe just as important as my search for the Whale culture that started in Greenland and brought me to the Pacific in search of the lost land of Mu.

The Petroglyphs on the Canary Islands had clearly shown what is known as the Eye of Africa or sometimes the Eye of the Sahara. Another common name is the Richat Structure. This clearly round geological ring structure is very visible from space and the Petroglyphs showed a very good depiction of it along with the coast of Africa. It was clear that these ancient people of the Canary and Cape Verde islands had come from the area of the Eye of Africa, so to learn more we now had to go there. Thankfully the petroglyphs showed us where to look specifically as the Eye is very large.

From what I have gathered until now some form of civilization must have arisen in and around the eye in the drying period that came at the end of the African humid period during the Holocene maximum. As the Sahara grasslands of the Holocene Maximum started to dry up and turn to desert, the population of the vast Saharan steppe started to gather near the major rivers, where the land was still lush, as we know from the Nile, where the ancient Egyptian civilization grew forth from the people, who made the Nile valley their home. Only the Nile is still there, but the late Saharan grasslands had many more rivers and lakes that are today long gone, but existed for a long time even after the African humid period.

The river fed from a lake further inland from the Richat structure and the mountain range of which the Eye is part must also have received precipitation that led into this river system. The river then ran into a delta system in what is now the desert coastline of northern Mauritania. From here the Richat culture could then sail up to the Canary Islands and down to Cape Verde explaining our findings there. The Eye itself would most likely have supported a number of internal lakes and rivers making it excellent for settling and quite a defensive stronghold if threatened from the outside. The river below could then have provided extra farmland, but in the Eye, there must also have been internal farmland in a wetter period!

It seems plausible that a culture could have developed here at around the same time as the Egyptians developed around the Nile. They might even have had contact with each other through caravans across the desert. Both civilizations would then have had their origin in the peoples of the Saharan savanna during the Holocene maximum and started their development into more evolved cultures during the drying that created the Sahara Desert. The main difference being that the culture of the Eye was cut short by the drying up of the river that is gone today, while the Nile continued flowing in Egypt. Thus, the culture of the Eye would have died out in its early stages, while Egypt continued to develop.

It will be interesting to see what we find when we arrive at the Eye. How far might they have developed before the Sahara Desert ended their civilization? And why did it also disappear on the Canary and Cape Verde Islands as only a few petroglyphs remain of their people there? That is what we hope to answer when we arrive at our destination. Hopefully, the rock carving maps that we found on the Canary Islands will lead us to useful findings as former archaeological expeditions to the Richat structure have failed to make any findings beyond stone tools and indications of Neolithic cultures. This does not mean that nothing is there, as the Eye is vast and one needs to know where to look. We hope that we know where to look!

We now drive alongside the edge of the highland of which the Eye is part. It is a desolate dry landscape burnt by the sun. It is a long drive and we have stayed the night quite a number of times along the way, but finally, we are arriving at our destination at the curved rim of the gigantic eye. Now we only need to go to the general area that we are shown to by our pictures of the petroglyphs. It is quite an impressive sight to arrive at this large regular structure in this highland ridge. We do not know what to expect, but we find a way into the Eye itself through its outer rim. It is a good thing that our vehicle is very well suited for rough terrain.

We arrive at the coordinates that we have calculated from the rock-carved map and step out of the car. First thing is to set up camp. Angelo and Elena start to set up the tents, while I unpack the car and bring the luggage to them. We three are a good team and have the camp up in no time. As it is late, we settle for supper and decide to start out exploring first thing in the morning.

After a good night's sleep, we commence exploring the area. It seems that there are ancient dried-out lake beds in the area. The Eye is well suited to retain water inside its ridges. The lakes must have once been fed by precipitation from evaporation from the river that must once have flowed near the Eye. This would have been an excellent and stable water supply for the people who once lived here and the ridges also provided cool shade from the sun, which would have lessened evaporation from inside the eye once the water had fallen there.

Only when the river was completely gone would this interior water system have lost its source of replenishment and slowly dried up, but it is quite possible that the culture of the Eye could have survived for quite some time after the loss of the river.

Firstly, we would need to find some trace of this culture, however. We started to look around the rock faces on the interior ridge in the hope of finding some petroglyphs like the ones we found on the Canary and Cape Verde Islands.

Our search was not met with much success from the onset. The rock walls seemed rather nondescript with little to be found. If there had been a civilization here, it had not left much of a mark. The only thing that struck a note was how level the rock floor seemed to be. Almost like it had been cleared to make a foundation, but there were no traces of buildings, only rocks that had fallen to the floor and sand that had accumulated on it.

Strange that the culture of the Eye should not have left any buildings? It did not make sense. Even if the Eye had been abandoned, where were the leftovers usually left by a culture? This was not like the whale culture of Greenland and the Pacific that had been built from ice and with products that had disappeared in the sea. A culture here at the Eye would have been based on stone as a material. Why was it then so empty?

Maybe our reading of the petroglyphs on the islands had been wrong. But even there, little else than the rock carvings had been there. As I mused over our lack of findings, Elena brought our attention to a ledge not that far above us. We all looked up at it. The rock wall behind it did look uncannily smooth, and as soon as we knew it was there, it could be seen from all of the surrounding area.

It did not take us long to decide that it was worth a look. Only we needed to get up there. Fortunately, Angelo is an excellent climber, so he quickly got his climbing gear and started his ascent. It did not take him long to get up there, and shortly after, he yelled, Heureka! He had found petroglyphs.

He threw down a rope ladder that he brought up with him, and Elena and I also ascended to the ledge. It was true! The entire surface of the wall behind the ledge was full of petroglyphs. We had found a library of the people of the Eye. We quickly noted the same round petroglyph of the Richat Structure that we had found on the islands. The regular circles of the Eye of the Sahara made for beautiful and recognizable petroglyphs.

There were a series of these petroglyphs that seemed to show a progression of the development of the culture in the Eye, with the grasslands of the surroundings receding more and more, giving way to the desert. This also showed the culture establishing itself within the Eye and evolving more and more.

Petroglyphs of buildings were also abundant, which caused wonder as ruins were completely absent in all directions. It was very strange that none were here. The rock-carved maps also showed the river that passed the Eye and, in the hinterland, a huge lake was carved out.

It is speculated that a large lake there, and in many other places in the Sahara, existed during the African Humid Period, along with a huge version of what is today, Lake Chad. The carvings made a clear case that this lake had truly been there further in from the Richat Structure. This lake would have been able to maintain the river and a water system for a long time after the drying of the Sahara had begun.

Only, unlike the Nile, this lake and river no longer flowed from an area that was replenished with water from the outside. So, a slow draining like the one seen today in Lake Chad would have been the result. Apparently, the Eye had been the center of a river civilization, with many smaller settlements and cities along the river, which again is strange as there are few findings of anything in the area where the river would have run.

Could it be buried in the sand? That might explain it in the lost river valley, but not here in the Eye, where the bedrock is visible. There must be another explanation! While considering this, we found the carvings of the Atlantic coastline. This was shown alongside petroglyphs that were clearly ships.

Here we could see the answer to the connection to the Canary and Cape Verde Islands! The ships had been cut into the rockface with great detail. Ships much in style with what is known from ancient Egypt could be seen among the petroglyphs. The long-dried-up river most likely had conditions for sailing similar to those of the Nile, where the heat of the desert causes winds that allow sailing against the current during the day, and in the other direction, you can simply glide along with the current.

The same would apply for the great interior lake that fed the river. Here it would be possible to go to the coast during the day, as the wind would be towards the coast due to hot air rising over land. The reverse would be true for the night, when the lake would be warmer, and thus rising air over the lake would draw in winds from the surrounding land, allowing for very predictable sailing on the river and lake.

Arriving at the Atlantic coast would be different. Near shore, the same night and day cycle would apply, but further out the westward trade winds, along with the Canary Current, would apply. This begs the question of how they sailed up against the wind and current to the Canary Islands. Did they keep near shore to use the day-night cycle winds?

Thus, we would need to seek answers among the petroglyphs. As we looked on through the rock carvings, we also found a great circle with lines going left at the bottom part and going right at the top! We were at the time not able to decipher this, but the carving was very large and was shown repeatedly on the wall, so it had to be significant. But it was different than the repeated circles that indicated the Eye of Africa itself, so it had to refer to something else.

We started out by looking at more petroglyphs signifying ships, as this tied in with our original discoveries on the Canary and Cape Verde Islands. They would have needed to have ships that could make the journey.

It would be reasonable to assume that the culture of the Eye would have gone to sea, as inland options would be scarce due to desertification. To the south would be the memory of the jungles of the African Humid Period, where the tsetse fly, with its diseases that attacked both people and especially livestock, would be a barrier. Then, like it would remain in later history.

So, going to sea in the Atlantic at the mouth of their river would make sense for the culture of the Eye, as the other still habitable areas in the drying Sahara would already be populated, like the Nile in Egypt.

We continued looking over the many, many petroglyphs covering the wall and started to find carvings of ships that looked larger and different from what we had just found. What struck out about these was that they seemed to have very high freeboard, making them more suitable for the open ocean.

What made such ships problematic in ancient times was that they are unsuitable to be rowed, as oarsmen need to be closer to the water for traditional rowing, explaining the low freeboard of Mediterranean galleys. Rowing was necessary in a time with less advanced sail riggings.

We did notice that the culture of the Eye seemed to have found a way around this, where they could still use oars despite the high freeboard. All the ships we found carved only had simple square rigging on a single mast, even if the sail seemed to be sometimes triangular with one end pointing down to the deck. This meant that they would need rowers for maneuvering in difficult waters.

They had solved the high freeboard problem in a novel way. At the top of the hull, they seemed to have had an overhang with room for oarsmen. The oars would then have gone straight down through a hole in the overhang floor. The oars would then, when in use, be connected to a form of crankshaft that the rowers would then turn. The edge of the hole in the floor would act as a counter to the oar stroke when the crankshaft crossed over its lowest point.

A quite ingenious but simple way of having both a high freeboard and the ability to row the ship. The oars could also be unmounted when not in use to keep them safe from damage. Each oar crankshaft seems to have been handled by at least two oarsmen.

This gave a pretty good idea of how they had managed to reach the Canary Islands. Northwards they would have had to go against the Canary current, so staying close to land, where the current is broken by friction with land and the prevailing trade winds are also interrupted by the night-day wind cycle of the desert, was preferable. However, it makes it necessary to move rather independently of the wind due to the primitive rigging.

Thus, the arrangement of the oarsmen would have been a great boon for the maneuverability of the ships in the Atlantic. The crew would have needed to be rather large to have enough oarsmen, so it is interesting what made the culture of the Eye interested in using these resources to sail out into the Atlantic. Maybe we would be able to ascertain this from further reading of the petroglyphs.

It seemed that the culture of the Eye became very affluent from the concentration of population in the river valley, and the Eye and desert provided protection from outside threats. The great lake seems to have maintained a water cycle good enough to keep the area suitable for agriculture, but it would not have had the seasonal inundation that is the boon of the Nile River.

So, nutrients would seem to have been actively brought in from what we can gather from the rock carvings. We saw many a petroglyph showing something being uploaded from the ships onto the fields.

Some were clearly rocks being pulverized and spread on the floodplains, while others were more elusive. It seemed to be a plant of some sort.

There were larger carvings of it, but we could not make out what it was. It seemed to be rather amorphous in its shape. Maybe we would find out as we became able to read more of the petroglyphs.

It seemed that the material brought in on the ships was also wood for building more ships. It was not that surprising considering that the mountains would have sparse wood coverage and much wood was needed for the ships. Now the question was, where they got the wood. The most likely source would be the West African rainforest along the coasts to the south, which could be reached from Cape Verde.

Maybe they also found the amorphous plant for fertilizing there? Another large input from this fleet of oceangoing ships is given by a large number of petroglyphs. A large part of the culture's animal diet must have been in the form of fish brought in from the Atlantic.

From the petroglyphs, it became clear that they had nets for fishing and were able to retrieve quite large catches from the sea. As the desert had encircled and isolated the culture of the Eye, they seem to increasingly have followed the river to the Atlantic and focused their outward activities towards the sea.

This does make sense since the distances across the desert from the Eye to anywhere else would have been very large. They might very well have had contact with Egypt on the other side of the Sahara, but the sheer size of the desert would have put a limit on this contact.

On the sea, the culture of the Eye might have had contact with the Mediterranean through the Strait of Gibraltar, but it remains to be seen whether the Eye was still inhabited by the time of Carthage or whether it was by then already abandoned. It might also be that the ships of the Eye never ventured as far as the Gibraltar Strait and given that Phoenician sources do not mention any maritime culture down the African Atlantic coast, it is very possible that the river had dried out at that time and the culture thus disappeared.

What we can read from the petroglyphs is that for a period these ships would have sailed on the Atlantic and brought needed resources back to the lush river valley that fed this lost civilization.

Angelo brings to our attention some map rock carvings that show the Eye at the center with the lake, river, and Atlantic coast around. It shows ships going up north to find fertilizing rocks. This might very well be phosphates from Western Sahara, which are still extremely important in modern agriculture. It ties in well with the Canary Islands as they lie off the coast of Western Sahara. They might have been an important stop for the transport of fertilizer.

Another route goes south, showing wood being brought in from the tropics as I assumed. It does make sense as this is the nearest source of wood that would have been available. It does not seem to have been traded. The people of the Eye seem to have cut the wood near the coast themselves and so too do they seem to have sent out people to mine the phosphate.

Thus, they had a somewhat isolated supply system owing to their very isolated position. Egypt in the east was close to many other cultures, while the culture of the Eye was very isolated, with only some nomadic people in the deserts around it, and the Malian kingdoms did not yet exist as the forest in the south had not yet withdrawn enough. Thus, the culture would primarily have evolved on its own.

What did get our attention on the rock map was a route that went straight out into the Atlantic along the trade winds! This was quite the revelation that this ancient culture could have sailed deep into the Atlantic following the same winds and currents that brought Columbus to the Americas.

The question then is whether they reached the Americas? The map shows no landmass or coastline in the route's direction. It does, however, show the strange amorphous plant used to fertilize the river valley.

This is quite interesting that they apparently got the plant from the Atlantic. Again, the great circular petroglyph is shown, and we start to realize what this is all about as the route seems to be circular around the great circle petroglyph and the plant is inside!

It must be the North Atlantic gyre. The great circular current system of the North Atlantic and within it is the Sargasso Sea, known for its large patches of floating sargassum algae. This is the plant that the culture of the Eye used to fertilize the river valley. They harvested Sargassum in the Sargasso Sea! It was quite the feat for an early civilization to build ships that could bring them this far out in the Atlantic!

From what we could make out, they used the trade winds and the North Atlantic gyre to go out and turned into the gyre to enter the Sargasso Sea, where they could then harvest sargassum. To go back home, they went back into the oceanic current of the gyre and followed it north into the Westerlies. That brought them back east, and the Canary current then brought them back south and home.

This is a level of knowledge of the oceanic currents and winds that would not come about again before the Age of Exploration. The fact that the ships of the culture of the Eye could be rowed was a great advantage both in the prevalent calm of the Sargasso Sea and when they would cross the horse latitudes, where the trade winds and westerlies separate and the weather, therefore, is also generally calm.

What we also notice in the great circle symbolizing the North Atlantic gyre are some dots set at specific areas. Now that we know that it symbolizes the gyre, we realize that these are the islands: Bermuda, the Azores, Madeira, the Canary Islands, and Cape Verde, the two last where we found the first trace of this remarkable culture.

It makes sense that if the culture of the Eye knew of the North Atlantic gyre, they would also know about the islands that the gyre flows past. These islands would give them places to stop and resupply. Water would most likely be especially needed after a long voyage, where the oarsmen would have had to do a lot of rowing in the stillness of the Sargasso Sea.

This is an astonishing development to think that this culture has been dependent on the harvesting of sargassum to maintain the fertility of their river valley. Aside from the sargassum, a large number of fish also seems to have been brought in, adding needed protein to the diet.

It seems that the fleets of the Eye set up an entire transportation network to bring in sargassum and fish from the sea, phosphates from Western Sahara, and wood from the mangroves to the south. While looking at the petroglyphs, it occurred to us that the delta of the river was a prime source of straw and rushes, and it seemed that they had been experimenting with making floating islands from straw and rushes and planting mangroves brought in from the south there to create a nearer source of wood.

From what we can tell, this was successful, and they started to be able to grow mangroves on these floating islands to expand their source of wood. This, in the end, meant that they no longer needed to go south to chop wood. The journey had become longer and longer as the woodlands retreated from the expansion of the Sahel grassland southward.

Thus, the culture of the Eye clearly sought to become less dependent on going to other land areas for resources. On the other hand, they did seem to have used more and more of the sea, venturing out to the Sargasso Sea inside the North Atlantic gyre. Only the phosphates from the North seemed to have remained for some time, but they, too, were slowly phased out for greater amounts of sargassum.

The artificial islands with mangroves and even agriculture, like what is known from pre-Columbian Mexico and Lake Titicaca in the Andes, seem to have grown in number. They are more and more prevalent among the petroglyphs.

The culture of the Eye must have become more and more adept at aquaculture as the desert encroached. It is impressive that they had become so good at aquaculture in salt water. From what we can tell from the petroglyphs, they used adapted triangular sails as moisture traps to catch water and lead it down to get fresh water.

Also, the main internal lake seems to have had its share of floating stands like the ones known from the Uru people in Lake Titicaca. This desert people became more and more aquatic as time passed and the desert spread. It seems that their architecture was mainly straw huts. Only in the Eye does it seem there were stone buildings, from what we can read from the petroglyphs.

Only where are these buildings or their ruins now? It makes sense that straw huts are gone, but stone should remain, and yet none has been found in the Richat structure. We would have to continue looking through the many rock carvings to figure out where the buildings might have disappeared to. They must have removed them at some point in time. Nothing else made sense. The culture of the Eye itself must have removed the buildings for whatever reason.

The nomadic peoples of the region after the river dried up would have had neither the inclination nor the possibility to remove stone buildings. That is when Elena found some petroglyphs that showed the beginning of the end of the culture of the Richat structure. What was carved was a great wave sweeping away the fields and huts of the river valley.

It was not the drying that ended the valley, but a flood! The great inland lake had a high elevation and was held back by geological formations. These had given way and led to a cataclysmic emptying of the lake into the river valley and out into the ocean, flooding the entire valley south of the Eye.

Only the Eye itself and the floating islands of the delta seem to have been spared. The Eye had a high enough elevation to be spared, and the floating islands could float, even though some must have been swept into the Atlantic. This must have been a world-changing cataclysm for the culture of the Eye, with massive losses of lives.

From what we can read from the petroglyphs, the river valley was never the same again, and the great lake was completely gone, drying up and becoming a desert. It seems that some water system remained at the Eye and the surrounding mountain ridge, flowing into the much-diminished river, with the drying now being chronic.

This was the much-reduced shape that the great flood left the culture of the Eye in. Although the petroglyphs had now become very exciting, it was starting to get dark, so we decided to return to camp and start again in the morning. We sat down around the campfire and started cooking the canned food. The weather was nice and calm with the stars shining down on us from a cloudless sky. Beans, vegetables, and Spam— all straight from the can.

It is surprisingly tasty when eaten in the fresh air. We are all alone here. It is strange to think that an entire culture once called this desolate place home. Today, it is so empty and silent. This place must once have been green and lush. Now, it is dry and sand-colored as far as the eye can see.

What horror it must have been for these people when the great lake broke through its barriers and thundered down through the river valley. The people here in the Eye could only have looked on in terror as their compatriots were swept away and their land devastated.

How did they rise from this, if they did? Was this how the culture of the Eye ended, or did they manage to hold on in the Eye and on the floating islands, using what river remained for some time before the desert that now surrounded it took over completely?

Those were the questions that we hoped further reading of the petroglyphs would answer. We all agreed that the Eye had shown us far more than we had expected when we went here from the Canary Islands. A long-forgotten and lost culture had been revealed to us.

We sat musing about our findings through the dark desert evening as we had our coffee before settling in for the night. How wonderful a thought that we had found so much on our trip here. The Eye of the Sahara had shown itself to be a treasure trove, if only one knew where to look.

We went to sleep full of expectation for the coming morning. We got up with the sunrise, and after a nice canned breakfast, we went back to the cliff with the petroglyphs, crawling up the rope ladder to the ledge.

It was a boon for us that the culture of the Eye had evidently been quite focused on carving down their history in a clear and easy-to-comprehend fashion. This might be a characteristic of a culture that had not fully formed a written language that was taught to an upper class.

It became clear that the culture of the Eye had been strong enough to survive the emptying of the great lake, but the survivors were a changed people. They seemed to be keenly aware that without the great lake to sustain a water cycle, the drying would only increase, so they needed to act while some water still remained.

It seems that the marshland at the delta of the river had quickly recovered and retained such a watery environment that straw and rushes quickly became abundant. With this resource, the people of the Eye doubled down on making more and more drought-resistant floating islands with water trap sails.

They thus started to build up an archipelago on and off the delta. What we then saw made sense regarding the complete absence of ruins in the Eye. The people of the Eye clearly understood that their homeland was dying with no possibility of recovering, so they started to dismantle the towns and cities in the Eye and load them onto the ships that could still travel as far as the Eye up the river.

They then brought the pieces to the new floating islands and rebuilt their culture on them.

This was amazing! This culture so long ago simply abandoned living on land to get out to live at sea on floating islands. Just like the Roman ruins were cannibalized for new buildings after the Roman Empire was no more, the culture of the Eye had simply reused the buildings in the Richat structure to build their new floating civilization.

This made sense as it is easier to reuse stone that has been cut than cut new stone in a society without power tools. Presumably, the ruins that should have been here at the Eye must now lie at the bottom of the ocean off the coast of Mauritania.

This was becoming quite exciting as it became more and more clear that the entire culture of the Eye was simply uprooted and moved onto the floating islands and that these islands got their water not from land, but from water collecting sails.

It was only the beginning, however, as the greatest discovery was now to come. Among the petroglyphs, it was clear that the river god was becoming an ocean god, but a god of the great oceanic river that is the North Atlantic gyre and the agricultural gods became more and more water gods.

Everything became more and more water oriented and the Sargassum became more and more revered as it was so important to the culture of the floating islands.

This is where we noticed the final shift in the culture of the Eye. The Atlantic off the coast of Mauritania can be rough and the distance to the sargassum of the Sargasso Sea is rather far. But they now lived on floating islands!

The petroglyphs showed the islands being set adrift to slowly float into the North Atlantic gyre and inwards to the calm waters of the Sargasso Sea. This process started out small, but it seems that, in the end, the entire floating culture moved to the Sargasso Sea!

This is where the petroglyphs stopped. There were no one left to carve new ones. Only a large petroglyph of the North Atlantic gyre with the islands Bermuda, the Azores, Madeira, the Canary Islands, and Cape Verde remained.

This is absolutely amazing: an island civilization in the middle of the Atlantic with old connections to Egypt. This meets the description of Atlantis by Plato! The culture of the Eye must have become the lost land of Atlantis and the fact that their islands were floating rather than solid explains why they have left so few traces.

Whatever befell them in the tragedy described by Plato, it would have left their remnants scattered on the abyssal plain deep beneath the surface of the Sargasso Sea many miles down. But as long as the Atlantean culture remained afloat, it could have had contact with the Mediterranean cultures through the Strait of Gibraltar.

How wonderful a thought to think of an entire culture resting on floating islands out in the Sargasso Sea. This is very akin to my findings of the whale culture of Mu in the Pacific. Only their floating civilization was earlier and rested on sea ice, but the late Mu culture of Zealandia did make floating islands and the last I found of them, they were set out to sea.

Maybe they settled in the south Pacific gyre like the Atlanteans settled inside the North Atlantic gyre. Both cultures ended up disappearing, however, only remaining in myth and legend. The latest I found of the Whale culture was also my first on the coast of Greenland, where they disappeared at about the time when the Atlanteans set out to settle the Sargasso Sea.

Such fascinating cultures of the ancient past. I still have to search for the remnants of the Whale cultures in South America on my to-do list, but for now, I will focus on this astonishing find of Atlantis.

Since the petroglyphs end here, we need to figure out what our next step will be. Around the campfire that evening we mused about how to proceed. For all that we had learned and the fact that we had most likely found the truth of Atlantis, we were at the same time stuck, since we had nowhere to go to look for the lost island, because these islands were floating and whatever leftovers would be scattered on the ocean floor or at the coasts of the North Atlantic.

All we had were the islands of Bermuda, the Azores, Madeira, the Canary Islands, and Cape Verde. We had already been to the Canary Islands and Cape Verde and they led us here. So that left us with Bermuda, the Azores, and Madeira. But where to look?

I knew of nothing that had been found on them that could help us. That is when Angelo mentioned an article he had once read about a place in Bermuda that seemed to have been a quarry, but no one knew for what or who had made it. This was our best lead and we decided to return to Nouakchott the next day and board l'Aguila again to sail to Bermuda.

As said so done, the day after we set off in the jeep through the desert on our way back to Nouakchott. Strange to think that the desert landscape around us once harbored a river that was the lifeblood of an entire culture that would replace it with the magic depths of the Atlantic.

The long-lost delta of this river was the large desert region just to the North of the capital. As it would take some time to arrive at our destination, we decided that we might as well take a little detour to look at this area. It did not really bring us much.

All that was there were endless windswept dunes. Nothing of the delta that would once have been was left. All had been blown away by the dust, so we headed back to Nouakchott.

BERMUDA

The day after returning and boarding l'Aguila again, we set out of the port and set sail on the trade winds out into the Atlantic as the proto-Atlanteans would have done, when they left what had once been their homeland.

I was happy to once again be aboard my lovely ship. It is nice to have the bopping water beneath one's feet and a nice wet saltiness in the air rather than the parched dryness of the desert air.

The wind filled our sails and we made good progress at sea following what would have been the route of the Atlanteans out along the southern part of the North Atlantic gyre. This meant that both the winds and the currents were on our side meaning that we sailed fast towards our destination.

Only unlike the Atlanteans, who would trail inward into the center of the Sargasso Sea, we would trail along the currents of the gyre at the rim of the sea to arrive at Bermuda.

Bermuda lies at the rim of the Sargasso Sea, so it is the most likely place to find hints of the floating Atlantis that the culture of the Eye would have built there. After having left their African homeland, it stands to reason that they would not have returned the long way there to quarry stone. They must only have disassembled their cities in the

Eye, while they could still sail the river, but after leaving with their floating islands for the Sargasso Sea the islands around the North Atlantic gyre would have been their only source of stone.

Much building would most likely have been done in organic materials that could be grown on the floating islands, but some stone might have been needed to maintain the buildings brought from the Eye and for more impressive buildings.

Since the weight mattered on floating islands, stone would most likely only have been used for important religious and public buildings. It would be interesting to see, if we could find something about how they constructed and maintained their floating islands after going to the Sargasso Sea, where they would need to get most of their resources from the floating islands themselves and the Sargassum harvested from the sea.

This would all remain to be seen. For now, we just followed the winds and currents to the west before going along with the northward gulf stream to Bermuda.

While on our way we had time to look into the quarry on Bermuda that Angelo had read about. It was not easy as very little information existed. It was clearly not something that had received much attention as most seemed to think that it was just a natural occurrence rather than man-made. That might be reasonable enough. We of course had reason to believe otherwise. Hopefully our much greater interest would yield findings in the quarry that no one else had even ever looked for.

Before long we reached Bermuda and sailed into the port of Hamilton, where l'Aguila would be our base of operation as we would go to the quarry during the day and return in the evening to stay the night aboard. A much nicer prospect than having to sleep in tents like at the Eye.

The day after we set out in a rented car to go to the quarry. After a bit of driving, not to mention wrong turns, we finally arrived at our destination. It quickly became clear that one could both assume that this was a man-made quarry as well as a naturally occurring phenomena.

The rock faces were squared out and straight as one would assume in a quarry, but at the same time it was overgrown and fell into the surroundings. We believed it to be a quarry, however, and set out to explore the area.

Luckily, we had it all to ourselves as the area did not seem to garner much interest from anyone else. It was rather nondescript to be honest, but then again quarries usually are not libraries!

We soldiered on and found absolutely nothing on this first day. On the drive back to l'Aguila we felt rather set back, but we decided to give it another go the next day. Hopefully fortune would be with us then.

It was not! We spent another day searching around the quarry only to find the strange squared off rock faces, but nothing else. So, it was for the day after and the day after again.

We found nothing to help us in our quest and frustration started to set in. We thus decided to drown our sorrows in rum at a local tavern. We might as well do so as continuing to search through the quarry was pointless.

That is where we fell in with some locals, who were happy to be bought some rum. We told them that we were looking for petroglyphs in the quarry, but had found nothing. That was when they asked if we had looked in the nearby tidal cave not that far from the quarry. It was known to have some rock carvings for divers to look at.

We immediately bought more rum and had them mark the cave on our map! We now had somewhere to go the next day.

We sailed out in l'Aguila and anchored up near the mouth of the tidal cave. It was a good natural harbor protected from the open ocean.

Angelo was quick to spot the upper part of the tidal cave. We had just passed high tide and were going to low tide, so the sea level was going our way. The cave could only be accessed from sea even at low tide, but then we would be able to sail in in our small dinghy.

This was not fast enough for Angelo, however, and he quickly got out his diving gear. I can dive, too, but am willing to wait to be able to sail in. Moments later Angelo dropped in. The impatience of youth, but at least we will soon know if anything is clearly visible in the cave.

Elena and I got to wait as Angelo swam off into the cave. I must admit to being anxious for the result. If Angelo finds nothing, we will be at a dead-end in our search for Atlantis.

He took his sweet time down in the cave, but we would need to wait for low tide anyway, but we started making use of the time by readying the dinghy for entering the cave. We believed that the time might indicate success.

Finally, we see Angelo surfacing again. He clearly indicated success and after getting on board again, he tells of his findings. There were carvings in the rock wall just above and below the surface at an area, where a ledge would probably be above water at low tide.

But this was not all! His most interesting find was that the cave continued further in with holes above. What he had found was that one led up to the quarry. The Atlanteans would have been able to lower rocks down from the quarry into rafts afloat in the cave. That would explain the complete lack of old roads into the quarry. Thus, the Atlanteans would have been able to bring out the rocks with the help of cave rafts. A rather ingenious solution actually and very much in tune with their floating culture.

We waited for the water to fall a bit further until Angelo thought that the ledge in the cave would be clear of the water. Then we sailed in with the dinghy. There is something awe-inspiring in entering a cave on the water just sailing into this gaping maw, where everything turns dark and cold. We could see the light coming down from the holes in the ceilings further in, however, so it was not all that dark. It did not take us long to get to the place, where Angelo pointed out the ledge that had just emerged from the water.

We quickly moored and disembarked to take a closer look at what was to be found. We set up a powerful light to help us see and as we lit it, we could immediately see the petroglyphs. As we scanned over them, we quickly recognized the circular shape of the North Atlantic gyre that we knew from the Eye of the Sahara. This was clear proof that we had found petroglyphs from the same culture.

What soon became clear was that these petroglyphs were made by the fully Atlantean culture after the great migration to the Sargasso Sea. This did make sense as this is when they would need an alternative source of stone, when living at sea. From what we could gather they never settled Bermuda, but only used it as an anchoring ground in the early days and later for the quarry. Their floating islands must have been a superior choice to settling the island.

What we noticed clearly from the petroglyphs was that they represented their homeland as a series of circles with openings giving almost a look like the Eye of Africa. But it was in the Sargasso Sea. They had simply arranged the core floating islands in a pattern of rings resembling the Eye. What this also clearly resembled was the description of Atlantis by Plato as a series of rings with canals inside. This just gave even more credibility to this being the true Atlantis placed on a floating island in the middle of the World Ocean.

From the petroglyph map and star markings it would seem that Atlantis would have been placed somewhere around the crossing of the longitude 60° West and the horse latitude 30° North right at the center of the Sargasso Sea. This would place it in the calm region of the horse latitude and at around the center of the rotating currents of the North Atlantic gyre. It would thus have been located sort of in the eye of the storm. This central area is constantly becalmed and would be a very safe place to locate floating islands and given the rotation of the ocean currents the islands would also be held there by the inwards force of the rotation. It made good sense that the Atlanteans would choose such a location for their floating civilization.

Even so, it might have been partially caused by nature rather than direct planning as the inwards rotation once inside the currents of the Sargasso Sea might have simply drifted them into this location. No matter the reason it was the ideal spot. From the other petroglyphs it was clear that both Bermuda, the Azores and Madeira were still islands that the Atlanteans visited, but it seemed that the Canary Islands and Cape Verde were by this time no longer in their sphere of influence.

The petroglyphs were also concerned with the quarry here and showing how the stone was brought to Atlantis to build the monumental buildings of the floating civilization. It must have been quite a sight to behold all these buildings standing tall on the otherwise flat floating islands on the calm sunny surface of the Sargasso Sea. The praising of the great buildings erected from the stones of the quarry was a continuous theme of the petroglyphs here in the cave, but suddenly the carvings simply stopped.

There was no warning. No indication of any problems or decline. The petroglyphs just showed the wonders of Atlantis in the Sargasso Sea and then no more petroglyphs! This did tie in well with Plato's description of the sudden catastrophic end of Atlantis. They simply never returned to the quarry here at Bermuda as Atlantis had sunk beneath the waves.

But it did leave us at a somewhat dead end. We needed to look closely at the petroglyphs to see if we could find any description of where to look for more on the Azores or Madeira to continue our search for more knowledge of the lost sunken Atlantis!

We looked through the petroglyphs and found much praise of the great floating civilization and the sun god that smiled from a cloudless sky. It was clear that both the Azores and Madeira were important. It did seem that some form of funeral necropolis was located in the Azores. The Atlanteans did not seem to be in favor of burial at sea as they were living at sea. So, they seemed to bring their dead to an island of the Azores for funeral pyres, but it was not clear which island was used.

That is when I remembered the megaliths researched by Dr. Rodrigues on Terceira Island. These megaliths indicated a culture thousands of years old that had existed on Terceira Island and there were indications of funeral pyres among these megaliths. Also, petroglyphs had been found on the island, so it would seem reasonable that this should be our next goal in the search for clues about the Atlanteans. This seems to be the natural next step so we packed up and left the cave before the tide started rising again.

We had already stocked up on supplies again before we left Hamilton, so we did not need to go back. We could leave directly for Terceira Island, but because it was late, we opted to stay anchored for the night and leave first thing in the morning. It feels a bit like returning home as I studied the megaliths of Terceira Island long ago as a young man. Back then not knowing that they might be related to anything like Atlantis as a floating island.

One of my favorite items from Terceira Island is the stone anchor blocks that can be found at the beaches with cut out holes with a diameter of 14 cm. The regularity of the diameter of these holes are a good indication that they are cut out by humans. These might then be anchor blocks from the Atlantean fleet visiting the island. I still have one of these stone anchors aboard l'Aguila as a memento of my trip there so long ago. Interesting how it has now become relevant again.

The next day we set sail and left Bermuda for the Azores. Just like the Atlanteans must have done, we go clockwise along with the gulf stream forming the upper part of the North Atlantic gyre. This way we have both the wind and currents with us as we go. The North Atlantic gyre forms a great wheel that you can sail along the southern part to go to America and then go up along the Northern part back to Europe. This most certainly would also have been the route used by the Atlanteans, when going around the Atlantic from their floating islands in the middle of the Sargasso Sea.

This would have allowed them to go almost anywhere in the North Atlantic. They would most likely have had to row their ships out from the calms of their floating homeland until they could use currents and winds to sail the North Atlantic. One can only imagine where they might have sailed to. They certainly had all the possibilities open to them.

It might very well be that they have had contact with the great bronze age kingdoms of the Mediterranean and might have traded with the Phoenicians, who are known to have left the Mediterranean to trade in tin for bronze alloys. Maybe the Atlanteans had some part in this trade? Their floating islands would not have had a source of copper or tin for bronze, so they might have imported it from the Eastern Mediterranean.

Then the question is what they might have had to trade for it? This for now is only speculation but some contact with the Mediterranean is certainly possible as the Atlanteans would have had historic memories of contact across the Sahara with Egypt.

THE AZORES

We were lucky to sail to the Azores in wonderful weather. The North Atlantic did not show us its teeth at all. We simply passed along quickly and chose to make a slight detour south into the Sargasso Sea, where we found large patches of Sargassum, which had been so valuable for the Atlanteans that it had in the end brought them from The Eye of Africa to their new home in the Sargasso Sea.

One cannot help but think that the position of Atlantis at 60° west and 30° North could still today be a place where boats and ships could congregate to create a floating community free of state dominance. Here a New Atlantis could thus be established by sea people freely sailing there and coming and going as they pleased. A community in constant flux, but with ships always there. These musings are certainly something that I will return to as a pillar of Institutio de la Vera. Maybe the other members of Le Club d'Aventure d'Outre-Mer will also find the idea of interest.

But for now, we must remain focused on our present project and leave the sargassum patches and go to Terceira Island and the picturesque capital of Angra do Heroísmo. It shall be a nice return to a place of my youth. The detour has added some time to our journey, but we are fast back on track.

We soon arrive at the port of Angra do Heroísmo, where we settle in and start preparing for our trip to the megaliths of the island and to the area, where petroglyphs are known to be. As I already know the area, we do not need as much preparation. We stayed the night in l'Aguila and rented a car the next day to go out to the megaliths. It is a vastly lusher landscape we drive through here than the desert in Mauritania and a much shorter distance, too. Like in Bermuda we will be able to return to l'Aguila each night.

Before long we arrive at the mysterious megaliths of Terceira Island. They are a strange wonder to behold and bring back memories of the past. It is speculated that these megaliths are related to those found in The British Isles, France and the Iberian Peninsula, which would indicate a culture capable of sailing the North Atlantic at a very early time. This fits in well with our research although we posit that the culture came from the sea to the land rather than the other way around. This would also fit in well with Atlantis having contact with the Mediterranean and being part of the Bronze age trade network.

As we arrive at the megaliths of Terceira Island, we quickly begin to search the area. Many petroglyphs have been found here through the years and I also remember some that I found here many years ago. This time, however, we know what we are looking for and have a reference from the petroglyphs that we have found on Bermuda, in the Eye of Africa and on the Canary Islands. We do not look for petroglyphs on the megaliths directly, but try to find megaliths that overlay cave walls, where we might find carvings done much like we saw earlier.

It takes us a couple of days, but finally we find a megalithic structure that has a cave-like crevice underneath and after entering we do find carvings on the walls around us. Elated we find the well-known circular petroglyph of the North Atlantic gyre. It looks exactly like the ones we have found before. There is no doubt that these are also Atlantean petroglyphs and not just a small amount like on Bermuda. This is a massive petroglyph wall. We have much work to do here!

It soon became clear that we had truly struck gold. The petroglyphs showed megaliths, ships and maps. With the prior knowledge that we had, we could clearly make out Bermuda, the Azores, Madeira, the Canary Islands and Cape Verde in the North Atlantic gyre. We could also see an outline of the coastline of Western Europe with Britain, Ireland, the French coast and the Iberian Peninsula. All the regions known for their megalithic structures.

Aside from these known islands and coastlines we could also see the large Archipelago at around 60° west and 30° south in the middle of the Sargasso Sea. These were the floating islands of Atlantis arranged in a circular pattern reminiscent of the Eye of Africa from where they had originated and that matched nicely with the description by Plato. They seemed to have built an entire oceanic empire from their location at the center of the Sargasso Sea.

From what we could make out they also knew of the Guyana coastline in South America and the Amazon delta, but like in their former African homeland they did not settle the tropical region, but seem to have gone there for harvesting wood. The dangers of tropical diseases must have also kept them out of South America. Most of their traveling and exports must thus have been focused on Europe and the Mediterranean.

From what can be read from the petroglyphs it becomes clear to us that the Atlanteans craved the bronze and other metal products that they could acquire from the bronze age kingdoms of the Mediterranean. There are many petroglyphs showing the trade for items seemingly of metal with a people, who must have been Phoenicians.

What now also starts to become clear is that the Atlanteans played a role in the trade network of the bronze production. Bronze is an alloy of copper and tin. Copper was available in the Eastern Mediterranean, but tin much less so. It could be found on the Iberian Peninsula and in Britain, however, which led to the formation of an extensive trade network to bring tin to the bronze age kingdoms for the production of bronze.

From the petroglyphs we gathered that the Atlanteans were involved in the extraction and transport of tin in both Britain and on the Iberian Peninsula. This was clearly important to them as they desired bronze, but could not make the alloy themselves. Many petroglyphs show base tin being exchanged for praised items in bronze, which are shown with great reverence.

It is not clear whether the Atlanteans did not know how to make bronze or whether they simply did not have access to copper for the alloy. Maybe it was both. Regardless they clearly needed to trade for it, which led them to be heavily engaged along the coasts of Western Europe. It is thus clear that Atlantis was a part of the Mediterranean bronze age world, which also explains how Plato could have heard of them from Egyptian sources. The Atlantean culture thus had connections across the entire North Atlantic and it expanded the reach of bronze age civilization significantly.

We are well aware of the significance of this. It must then also mean that a large number of bronze artifacts should now lie on the abyssal plains deep beneath the surface of the Sargasso Sea. A find of these artifacts down there would be proof that Atlantis had floated at the surface of the sea during the bronze Age. As we do not have the means to search the seafloor so for the time being we can only continue to read through the petroglyphs that are currently providing us with much information.

We now find an entire section with carvings showing the splendor of Atlantis. Massive structures of stone standing in the ocean under a sunny sky. Thousands of dew-catching sails providing fresh water for the floating civilization. There are fields and forests that float on the water providing the needs of the populace. It does, however, seem that more and more buildings of stone were added to the floating islands as the affluence grew.

And where the islands had once floated separately, they seem to over time have been connected with bridges or coupled directly together forming a single floating continent with a huge city cut through with canals to form the massive round harbor structure. It must have been quite the sight to behold! The petroglyphs show a temple of great significance at the center of the floating city. In this temple a massive statue of the Atlanteans sea god is depicted. This fits with Plato's description of Atlantis being beholden to Poseidon.

It makes sense that an ocean god would be central to a floating civilization. The ocean god had many depictions in the petroglyphs, often shown as being raised on columns standing tall above the hall of the temple, with a pond representing the ocean beneath it. In its hand was shown in the petroglyphs a miniature of Atlantis, so the ocean god could watch over its floating civilization.

The many centuries floating on the surface of the Sargasso Sea had given the Atlanteans a very close attachment to their ocean home, with their fleet being their pride. In the petroglyphs, many ships are depicted with their special rowing arrangement, which made it possible to row in and out of the windless center of the Sargasso Sea. Then, when reaching the North Atlantic gyre and the prevailing winds, the sails could be raised and the ships could reach all over the North Atlantic.

It was clear that this fleet became more and more important to the Atlanteans, who increasingly showed the fleet bringing in riches from land to their floating home. Less and less of the floating islands were used for trees and farming, as they were built with wood imported from the Amazon, like their forefathers had done from the African jungles. From Europe, it seemed that, aside from bronze and metal works, food was increasingly being imported rather than being grown.

The Atlanteans had become shippers of goods rather than producers and seemed to benefit greatly from this arrangement. They had truly become a sea people. Only continued harvesting of sargassum and fishing seemed to still be held in great esteem, as fish and sargassum petroglyphs were still common and seemed to be sold to trading partners at the European costs and in the Mediterranean. I guess the nutrient value of sargassum was appreciated by the Bronze Age kingdoms as a fertilizer, just as the people of the Eye had used it in Africa before the desert forced them to the sea, where they would become the Atlanteans.

It becomes more and more clear from the treasure trove of information that these petroglyphs are that Atlantis was a part of the Bronze Age trade network with contacts deep into the Mediterranean. This also explains the many accounts of this kingdom existing far out in the middle of the world ocean. What remains then is the fact that the accounts become something of the past with the end of the Bronze Age.

In the Iron Age and the Greek archaic and classical periods, the tales of Atlantis are of a kingdom that no longer exists. Something must have happened to Atlantis at the end of the Bronze Age, leading to its complete disappearance. With any luck, some of these petroglyphs might tell us something about what this cataclysmic event might have been that ended the floating islands of Atlantis. We did not immediately find anything to answer our questions.

The petroglyphs carried on lauding the greatness of Atlantis and the greatness of its navy. Especially the ocean god became more and more prevalent, showing it grant its blessings upon Atlantis, with the other gods, including the sun god, becoming subservient to him. It also seemed that, in the self-image of Atlantis, the land dwellers also became subjects to Atlantis, and the trade was being viewed as tribute from lesser vassals to the might of the ocean god's chosen.

One clear aspect of this that was clear from the petroglyphs was the increased building of massive stone buildings and statues on the floating island of Atlantis. The Atlanteans seemed to live in an increasing state of opulence, wanting to show it and honor their ocean god with many edifices. Thus, the quarrying of stone from Bermuda and the Azores intensified.

The glory of Atlantis at this time must have been reaching its zenith, with its mighty cities standing tall on the ocean surface, and their fleets sailing far and wide across the oceans, far beyond the known world of their Bronze Age trading partners. And then... the petroglyphs stop.

From what we can tell, the petroglyphs here only tell of the glory days of Atlantis, with nothing coming after—just the power and strength of the ocean kingdom and all its floating wonders in the Sargasso Sea, but nothing about what happened to this mighty civilization. There are no petroglyphs confirming Plato's account of the kingdom of Atlantis sinking into the sea. We would need to trail back through the rock carvings to find something that could help us go further.

It is evident that Atlantis and the floating islands must have sunk, but it is the how and why that interests us now. We went back through the petroglyphs, but nothing really caught our eyes. We could not find anything that would bring us further. Of course, it would be easier if we painted the petroglyphs to make them more visible, like I once did when researching the whale culture of Greenland.

Here, I painted all the petroglyphs to get a clear view. My search for the whale culture eventually led me to the Pacific, where I found evidence that the whale culture descended from the ice continent of Mu that had existed in the Pacific during the Ice Age. Here, the petroglyphs we found were submerged, so they could not be painted. We thus photographed them and used artificial intelligence to make the petroglyphs more visible and to find variations.

This was the solution here! We agreed to photograph and film all the petroglyphs here and then run them through the AI back aboard l'Aguila. Then the AI might be able to show us something that we were unable to see. We did so and returned back to Angra do Heroísmo and l'Aguila.

It was nice to be back aboard after some days at the megaliths. We could become civilized again with the amenities that my ship offered. She has, through the years, evolved into my true home more than my villa, which I do not live in as much as aboard l'Aguila.

As we settled in, we fed our photos and film to the AI and allowed it to start working its magic. Meanwhile, we could get some rest and think about all we had learned so far. This had been a wonderful journey, fully on par with my search for the land of Mu in the Pacific. It fills me with wonder how much of human history has been lost to the tides of time.

One can only wonder how much still lies unfound and unexplored in the depths of time and how the sheer alien nature of these lost cultures might affect how we live in the future. Might there one day again be humans living on the surface of the Sargasso Sea calling it home? Could we become seaborne nomads, using our boats and ships as floating homes on the surface of the ocean? Only time will tell.

For now, we would look back in time at what the AI could show us. The processing had finished, and we could finally sit down and look at what it had to show us. The pictures and film had been improved markedly, and the petroglyphs now showed clearly with all the fantastic imagery of Atlantis in its heyday. It seemed that all the petroglyphs had been carved in the same style and were generally of a high quality with clear lines and good craftsmanship. It was clearly made by a culture wanting to commemorate itself.

The AI showed us the images of the floating island of Atlantis in all its splendor with towering buildings atop. All showed the glory of the people at their peak. But then there was one single piece that stood out as not fitting in with the rest! Or rather, a single large petroglyph had been modified by someone, who was clearly not a craftsman of the same league as those who had made the other petroglyphs.

The AI showed us the by now very well-known circle representing the North Atlantic gyre with the Sargasso Sea inside, along with Atlantis. It also showed the positions of Bermuda, the Azores, Madeira, the Canary Islands, and Cape Verde. All this was in the usual style, but the image of Atlantis had been carved over with a tilted building sinking into waves, with ships all around and what seemed to be an arrow pointing to Madeira. Below was a simple carving showing the

Madeira archipelago clearly to those who know it. It showed Madeira itself, Porto Santos, and Desertas.

This made something dawn upon us, and Elena was the first to put it into words. If Atlantis had indeed sunk beneath the waves for whatever reason, the fleet would still be there, at least in part, and it might have saved any survivors from the sinking of Atlantis. Any fleeing ships going east would then go up into the eastward northern current of the North Atlantic gyre, and the first land they would reach would be the Azores.

These crude petroglyphs are a message to any stragglers that the bulk of the fleet had continued to Madeira and would be waiting for as long as possible for any remaining ships. What would be of the Atlantean refugees trying to keep their people together and regroup to survive post-Atlantis? They seem to have chosen Madeira as their new center of operation, and it is there that we too would need to go to find out more about what happened to Atlantis and maybe where the surviving Atlanteans went.

But we would need to look closer at the map petroglyph to find a more specific location. After studying the map of the Madeira archipelago closer, we found that the AI had highlighted a mark showing ships at Porto Santos, indicating that this island was the chosen gathering point of the Atlantean fleet. It seemed a bit strange that it would not be the larger main island of Madeira, but I remember having read an article regarding the localization of the ruins of ancient megalithic structures near water sources on Porto Santos, which matched up well with this island having importance.

But we still needed to know where on the island to look, so we had the AI mark up positions on Porto Santos by combining a map of the island with the petroglyph map. What came up was a location on the eastern side of the southern tip of the island, just off Miradouro das Flores and the smaller southern island Ilheu da Cal. This would be our next target. It was clear that this was where the ancient carved map directed its readers to.

The day after, we set out from Terceira Island and the Azores. We decided to go to Funchal on Madeira's main island to visit my villa there for some rest and relaxation and to unload some of our artifacts and findings in storage there. I have had my vacation villa on Madeira for many years and visit it from time to time to enjoy the island and spend some time reading in a relaxing environment. My Portuguese is good enough for me to live there in a not-too-touristy fashion, and I looked forward to seeing the villa again. As I only visit it from time to time, I have it looked after by a local cleaning and service company, so it is always ready for when I decide to go there.

PORTO SANTOS ISLAND, MADEIRA

After an uneventful voyage at sea, we arrived at the marina of Funchal, where I had a reserved spot for l'Aguila. We went ashore and hired a small van to load our findings and artifacts onto. Shortly thereafter, we were driving up to my villa. We quickly settled in with Angelo and Elena getting their rooms, and we started to order the artifacts and register them for storage.

Porto Santos and the continuation of our voyage for the tale of Atlantis did pull on us, but it was nice with a break, and the artifacts did need to be stored. Besides, the remnants of Atlantis on Porto Santos had been there for so long, so they could probably wait a little longer. We spent a couple of days ordering and categorizing everything and then rested a day or two afterward with nice dinners and time for some reading before we were ready to depart for the next leg of our journey.

I locked up the villa and we returned to l'Aguila and set sails for the short trip up to Porto Santos. The eastern side of the island has beautiful sandy beaches, while the western side is much more rugged. I imagine the Atlantean fleet being beached here, while they were gathering from the second disaster of their history. First, the desert swallowed their home at the Eye, and then the ocean swallowed Atlantis, with its remnants most likely scattered across the Abyssal plain beneath the Sargasso Sea.

We went to Vila Baleira, the largest city on the island, where we anchored l'Aguila and went ashore on Porto Santo Island. We rented a car to take us down the coast to Miradouro das Flores, where we would start searching for anything that could lead us to more petroglyphs that could tell us the continuation of the story of Atlantis.

We arrived at the beautiful site with a splendid view of Ilheu da Cal. We started searching around the area and did find what could be megalithic structures, but petroglyphs eluded us. This continued for days. We went out and searched through the southern tip of Porto Santos and found nothing remotely like a petroglyph. We did attract attention from tourists, though, who were curious as to what we were looking for. We made quite a spectacle, I am sure, but still, we found nothing of interest. We were disappointed.

Had the Atlantean fleet come here, but chosen not to leave any markings for stragglers? Or had they, in the end, never arrived? Questions, questions, but no answers. It became clear that we would find nothing by continuing to look in vain. No, we decided that we would have to ask around among the locals if any stones with carvings were known on the island. Fortunately, we all spoke some Portuguese, so we could each go around asking.

The next day we started going around trying to find anyone who might know about petroglyphs on the island! I had little luck through the day, and when I met Angelo again, it was clear that he, too, had failed. Elena, however, came smiling to us. She had gone to the local archive, and here some elderly volunteers had known about petroglyphs on Ilheu da Cal. They had old pictures of them that Elena was allowed to copy, and they had given her a map of Ilheu da Cal with an X, where the petroglyphs were.

The X marks the spot! So, the Atlanteans had cut the petroglyphs on this southern island. No wonder we had found nothing. I did wonder why there, but maybe it had some significance that we did not know of. We now had somewhere to go, and the next day we left Vila Baleira for the short trip to Ilheu da Cal.

We found a spot where l'Aguila could anchor and took the small boat ashore. Once on land, we started our walk upwards on the cliffs. The petroglyphs were up high on the rocky island. As we reached the cliff with the petroglyphs, what struck us was not the petroglyphs, but the view. It immediately made perfect sense to us why this place was chosen for the petroglyphs. The view was fantastic and strategically perfect.

You could see up both sides of Porto Santo Island with a great view of the beach, where the fleet would have been, and you could see up the rocky western side of the island, too. So, when you had a lookout here, an enemy would not be able to sneak in on you. There was also a great view across the Atlantic and over the sea towards Europe, making it almost impossible for anyone to close in unseen. We stood there for a short while, breath taken by the sight.

Then we remembered why we had come and turned our attention to the cliff with petroglyphs. It was massive! It quickly became clear that this was not only fast-made petroglyphs by members of the fleet after the sinking of Atlantis, but an entire era cut in stone, and somewhere the end of the way was to be found.

Quickly we found the well-known circular shape of the North Atlantic gyre with the floating islands of Atlantis in the Sargasso Sea in the middle, with Bermuda, the Azores, Madeira, the Canaries, and Cape Verde marked out. Also prominent were petroglyphs showing Atlantis in its heyday, with thousands of dew-catching sails shown prominently all over the magnificent city and island. This had been their source of fresh water, catching the dew of the ocean as it settled from evaporation in the morning and evening.

This seems to have been given special attention here, as Porto Santo was also shown with thousands of sails catching the morning dew. This makes sense, as Porto Santo lacks the height of Madeira that causes water to fall on this island, making it lush. Porto Santo tends to have droughts, so the use of dew sails must have been important for the Atlanteans here.

Indeed, petroglyphs of the island covered in dew sails are quite prevalent. This must have been a method for making the island lush and moist even though it is quite dry in its natural state. The dew sails must have been all important for Atlantis as they would have been the only way for the floating islands to gain fresh water from the surroundings.

It is quite likely that the dew sails are an old development from the culture of the Eye as the evermore dry conditions of the Sahara must have brought along developments that could generate more fresh water especially near the Atlantic coast, where dew, mist and fog could be trapped by the dew sails. The dew sails might thus have come to Porto Santo Island as early as with the first explorers from the culture of the Eye and indeed might simply have carried over, when it became the Atlantean culture.

The petroglyphs do seem to be ordered by period with distinct sections along the face of the cliff. They seem to have been carved from top down and from right to left meaning that the oldest are at the far-right side of the cliff. A quick overlook of the petroglyphs also shows that the glyph of the Eye of the Sahara features prominently in the right section, while the great ring of the North Atlantic gyre starts to appear later and on the second half of the cliff the floating islands of Atlantis appear inside the great ring.

Also very notable is that the floating islands of Atlantis were arranged in a shape reminiscent of the circular rings of the Eye of the Sahara. A legacy of their original home no doubt. The cliff does show much of the early history with the culture of the Eye indicating that Madeira and Porto Santo Island must have been settled early in the history of the culture, while they were exploring the North Atlantic gyre and the Sargasso Sea to find the Sargassum that would be so important to their culture.

From what we can tell from these petroglyphs the Canary Islands were the first islands to be found by the culture of the Eye as they established a sea route to the phosphate mines of Western Sahara. They seem to have originally had a land route, but by going up close to the coast they could reach up by sea despite the Canary current and then go back by the same current and thus they discovered the Canary Islands on the home trip.

Due to the difficulty of going up against the current, the culture of the Eye would then try different routes out to sea until they discovered the Volta do Mar, which the Portuguese would rediscover millennia later. The Volta do Mar would bring the culture of the Eye to the Azores and Madeira as it later did the Portuguese. Cape Verde would be found by following the current out from the delta in Mauritania.

From here mistakes and curiosity would bring them further out into the North Atlantic gyre and into the stillness of the Sargasso Sea, where they would find the Sargassum that would become another important fertilizer for their agriculture and later the base material for growing food on their floating islands. The petroglyphs show the islands spreading out from the long-lost delta in Mauritania and how they tried to establish floating islands near Madeira, the Azores and Canary Islands, but the weather and currents proved problematic so the islands were established further into the stillness of the Sargasso Sea, where they would be less threatened by the elements and closer to the valuable sargassum harvest. And Atlantis was born in the middle of the ocean.

Then comes many of the same scenes that we also found up in the Azores of mighty Atlantis floating upon the waves protected by their great sea god in his temple in the center of the ringed floating islands. Here even more than on the Azores we also see petroglyphs showing the trade with the Mediterranean cultures, which makes sense as Madeira would be the gate between the sea surrounded by ocean, the Sargasso, and the sea surrounded by land the Mediterranean.

The Atlanteans here on Porto Santo Island clearly were more influenced by the bronze age cultures of the Mediterranean and the petroglyphs show many images of the splendors of the land dwellers. We noted petroglyphs that were clearly references to the pyramids of Egypt and Babylonian ziggurats. Also, petroglyphs of large land cities are shown. Here they clearly also revered the Mediterranean cultures and knew much about them.

Many petroglyphs also show the riches that were traded with the great bronze age kingdoms; bronze and copper tools, great vessels of bronze and pottery. Basically, all the things made from raw materials that were only available on land. The petroglyphs also show another sea people that the Atlanteans traded all these items with in exchange for tin that was bought in from Britain and the French and Iberian Atlantic coasts for bronze works.

It seems that Porto Santo Island and Madeira were great hubs for this very lucrative trade, which also included products from Atlantis itself. Mainly products that could be grown on the floating islands and sargassum, but it also seems that seashell, turtle shells and pearls were valuable commodities. I would assume that the other seafaring culture with which the Atlanteans traded would have been the Phoenicians as these were important in the trade network that supplied tin to bronze and were established as far as the Iberian Peninsula.

This would make it likely that they had contact and the Atlanteans would have been able to get the tin from especially Britain to the Phoenicians around middlemen on the European mainland. There thus might very well have been a basis for mutually beneficial trade between the Atlanteans and Phoenicians. From one sea people to another.

This segment of the petroglyphs does show this other sea people quite prominently indicating a lively contact with the Atlanteans of Madeira and much cultural exchange between them. They might have taught the Atlanteans much about the great bronze age kingdoms of the Eastern Mediterranean and some Atlanteans might even have voyaged there together with Phoenician merchants to visit the great bronze age cities, which would rival their own Atlantis.

This cultural exchange would then have left the memory of the great city in the ocean that Plato would describe centuries later. From this perspective it would make sense that Madeira and Porto Santo Island would have been a hub for trade between Atlantis and the Mediterranean world with the Phoenicians acting as middlemen in an extensive trade network that bound the Atlantic to the Mediterranean.

This also shines light on why the Atlantean fleet would go here after the fall of Atlantis as this would be the main hub connecting to other large cultures that the Atlanteans had close connection to. Then the main question arises; what did the Atlantean fleet do after gathering here? This is something that we will hopefully find some answer to among these petroglyphs.

Unfortunately, reading from the last part of the cliff wall, which should be the youngest, only shows Atlantis at its zenith. If the members of the fleet carved a message on this wall, they must have done so elsewhere. We will need to look through all of it to see if there is a message.

Luckily, we saw on the Azores that the craftsmanship is not quite the same on the new petroglyphs, so this is what we need to look for. While looking, we found a map of the North Atlantic gyre like those we had seen often before, but this also showed European coastlines and, to our surprise, coastlines at the other side, too.

So, the Atlanteans had also mapped out the American east coast. It was not only the South American Guinea coasts from where they got lumber that they mapped. They also knew of the North American coastlines. This shows the massive extent of the Atlanteans' knowledge of the North Atlantic.

It did not seem that they had done any settling of the American coast, however, their trade seems to have been focused on the evolved bronze age kingdoms of the Mediterranean and the acquisition of tin from Britain to trade with there. Maybe the Atlanteans simply did not find anything that they wanted on the North American coastlines and thus let them be?

Perhaps the inland nature of most advanced cultures in the Americas meant that the Atlanteans only established very limited contact in America, while the coastal and maritime nature of the Mediterranean cultures led to much more extensive contact and trade. This might very well be and as the Atlanteans seem to have preferred to stay at sea, they would not have settled the American coastlines and established much inland contact.

They seem to have focused their outside contact on the Mediterranean cultures. This at least is what the petroglyphs would seem to indicate as most voyages are depicted as going to the Mediterranean and the British Isles.

As we stood there musing over all that these petroglyphs showed us, Angelo suddenly brought our attention to a section that he had been looking at somewhere in the middle of the wall. When Elena and I had come, he pointed to a large petroglyph of the by now well-known North Atlantic gyre with the floating continent of Atlantis inside.

It was not this glyph itself that he called our attention to, but the fact that a massive crack had been cut down through it. Below, less well-made scribbled petroglyphs had been cut. This was clearly it! These were inscriptions made by the surviving Atlantean fleet!

The crack through the great circular glyph clearly pointed to the great fall of Atlantis and the smaller petroglyphs below told the story of this fall. It showed how the kings of Atlantis had garnered the wrath of their great sea god by covering more and more of his ocean with floating islands and how they had brought more and more land in the form of stone out unto the sea so that in the end, the sea god had swallowed it all in one terrible event.

Oh my god, that is it! The Atlanteans had connected the islands and then built so much stone atop of them that in the end, they simply became too heavy and sank in one fell moment, ending their floating civilization. Truly an ending through a culture's own hubris just as described by Plato.

The Atlanteans had forgotten that their islands needed to be able to float! Such an ironic end to a marine civilization! The scribbled petroglyphs then show the fleet saving who they could from the water of the vengeful sea god and then fleeing his wrath in terror, gathering here at Porto Santo Island and Madeira to find some footing and plan an escape.

Clearly, the few islands could not support the many refugees in the fleet, so they quickly became depleted. Both Bermuda, the Azores, the Canary Islands, Cape Verde, and at last Madeira would be abandoned. The Atlanteans still had to flee the vengeance of their sea god.

As the sun god had once driven them from the Eye of the Sahara to the sea, now the sea god drove them towards land. They knew of only one area where the cultures were advanced enough for their numbers, and that was the Mediterranean cultures. The petroglyphs show their ships sailing into the Mediterranean. A message to any stragglers to follow their kinsmen to where they hoped to find salvation from the wrath of their sea god trying to punish their hubris.

Their fleet was armed as the survivors were mostly young, fighting able men that could take what they needed if not given willingly to help the refugees. That is when it dawned on me, who the Atlanteans became! This was at the end of the Bronze Age and the Atlantean fleet suddenly arrived filled with warriors.

The Atlanteans were the mysterious sea peoples of the bronze age collapse! So, in the end, the Atlanteans would be part of the chain of events that brought doom to the bronze age kingdoms and as they were an integral part of the trade network that supplied the metals needed to make bronze, their later absence from the Atlantic would also mean a missing link in the bronze age trade network.

Thus, the fall of Atlantis would be part of the chain of events that would also mean the fall of the bronze age kingdoms and the beginning of the more insulated Iron Age, where the trade networks would take centuries to rebuild. No doubt the deluge of the Atlantean fleet entering the Mediterranean would drag along other peoples, whose livelihood had disappeared, further adding to the stream of sea peoples going east.

It then comes to my mind that the biblical Philistines and their sea god Dagon, whose temple would be tumbled by Samson, were very likely a group of Atlantean sea people having settled in the south of Israel. This would explain their mysterious origin as they seem to have simply manifested from out of nowhere at the beginning of the Iron Age, becoming the main enemy of the Israelites for a long period, where they seem to have established themselves as a ruling warrior class.

Since the Atlantean fleet would to a large extent consist of the armed men of Atlantis, it seems reasonable that they would establish themselves as an armed ruling class, where they arrived as conquerors. The Atlanteans would thus end as a conquering class in the ancient near east, where they would rule their former trading partners until they would be toppled by those they oppressed as Samson toppled their sea god Dagon.

This fits well with the superior attitude towards the bronze age kingdoms that we found evident in the petroglyphs in the Azores and here in Madeira. They already felt as masters before entering the Mediterranean as conquerors.

And so, they arrived as a horde on the coast of the great bronze age kingdoms, both destroying the kingdoms and the intricate trade network that had sustained them and of which the Atlantean sea people had themselves originally been part. This process led to a complete rearrangement of the Mediterranean world with the sprawling cities of the bronze age kingdoms retreating behind walls of smaller defensible fortress cities, often placed high in the landscape far from the threatening sea.

This would be the lasting legacy of the Atlantean retreat from the sea. The sea god's wrath went far in from the coast. Some of these new fortress cities would be ruled by the Atlantean sea people like those of the Philistines, while others would be defended by the peoples that were attacked by them.

Along their way through the Mediterranean, the Atlantean fleet most likely gathered others around them as they plundered the coasts to sustain themselves. This set in motion a large migration towards the east. Maybe some Atlantean ships settled further west in the Mediterranean with parts of the peoples there being dragged along east.

As the sea peoples of the bronze age collapse did not establish a large coherent empire, but only regional small powers like the Philistines, it does suggest that the Atlantean refugees and those that followed them did not maintain a system of command, but simply became a wave of individual ships and captains seeking their own fortune. Thus, creating a wave of plunder and settlements all across the Mediterranean, spreading their heritage throughout.

This more or less brings us full circle. The culture that was established at the Eye of Africa during the desertification of the Sahara would be driven to sea by the encroaching sand and here would establish the legendary kingdom of Atlantis, which would rule the waves of the North Atlantic and establish trade connections with the bronze age kingdoms in the Levant, thus making contact with Egypt—another culture that emerged from the desertification of the Sahara. Only the Nile did not dry out, so Egypt would remain.

Then, when the hubris of Atlantis led them to overbuild on the floating island of their kingdom, it all sank beneath the waves on one single fateful day, leaving only the Atlantean fleet, which then set sail to assault their former trading partners in the Mediterranean, thus contributing to the bronze age collapse.

The remaining survivors of Atlantis would thus establish a number of small kingdoms in the Mediterranean that would then be absorbed into the general Mediterranean peoples, but leaving the cultural memory of the great oceanic kingdom that would be swallowed by the sea. The Atlanteans thus not only linger as a cultural memory in the

Mediterranean and Europe but have also left a genetic mark by being absorbed into the populations over time.

Thus, the Atlanteans are not truly lost but live on in the peoples that they once invaded from the sea. Both Angelo, Elena, and I are moved by what we have found and happy to have made this journey of discovery full circle.

If we are to make any further investigation, it will have to be research of the areas where the sea peoples arrived in the Mediterranean after the fall of Atlantis. But this will have to be a journey for another day. We are for now satisfied with what we have found and how we were able to follow the evolution of the Atlantean culture through its birth at the Eye of Africa to its Atlantic maturity and its ending in the Mediterranean.

What is very interesting to me is that this is the second culture moving entirely unto the sea that I have explored. My long travels and search for the whale culture that I first found evidence of in Greenland led me into the Pacific, where underwater petroglyphs showed that this culture had existed on a massive ice cover that came up from the Antarctic along the Humboldt current and into the Pacific during the ice age. This ice cover was almost like the lost continent of Mu.

This culture of Mu existed almost entirely at sea on the ice cover, hunting whales and seals from airships. I even found evidence that the Mu culture had built floating islands of reeds from swamplands as the ice receded to continue their maritime culture. Thus, two cultures separated by millennia both took to the sea and established artificial floating islands in the ocean to live there.

I therefore now have two completely separate pieces of evidence of humans settling the ocean. One can then only ask whether these are the only examples or whether other fully oceanic cultures might have existed?

In some ways, one could argue that the Austronesian and especially the Polynesian cultures are a current example of almost fully maritime cultures. Even though they live on actual islands, they have their main activity at sea. And in the Arctic, the Inuit lived on the ice cover and hunted sea mammals, being fully dependent on the ocean.

So, there are more examples, and one might then imagine that we could one day again establish a larger cultural presence at sea instead of just passing across it. It does, however, necessitate building a culture that is dependent on the ocean and to live there to maintain itself. This would be what is needed for such a culture to arise. A culture needs to exist where it has a source of sustenance.

These are all musings, but given the evidence of cultures wholly based on the ocean, it should not be a stretch to envision that something similar could come about again.

After having photographed the entire cliff here on Ilheu da Cal and returning back down to l'Aguila, we felt that we had completed our journey and opted to sail back to Madeira proper to my Villa in Funchal. Here, we got some rest and ordered our photos of the cliff on Ilheu da Cal to set all our findings together to make a coherent timeline of the culture of the Eye and its evolution into Atlantis.

Then from there to the Atlanteans' sudden transformation into the sea peoples and their flood into the Mediterranean. Our journey was, as such, at an end, but we did feel that something was missing. Not in the sense that we missed something in the story that we had pieced together, but that we still missed a visit to an important place in the story.

THE SARAGASSO SEA

This was the site of Atlantis itself. After some days all three of us agreed that we needed to finish this voyage by going to the Sargasso Sea to see where the floating islands of Atlantis must have once floated.

The day after, we packed up and sailed out of Funchal. We followed the Canary current and the North Atlantic current south and west, closing inwards to the Sargasso Sea.

As we ventured inwards, the winds and currents subsided as we closed in on the coordinates 30° North and 60° West. Soon the sea was so calm that we had to rely on l'Aguila's engine entirely. Large patches of the, to Atlantis, all-important Sargassum greeted us.

There truly is something eerie about this calm sea overgrown with these algae. One almost feels like it grows towards the ship. It wasn't a problem, however, but I can see how unnerving it would be to crews entirely reliant on wind and current to be stuck here.

That is why the Atlanteans used oars, too!

As we finally reached our destination at the crossing of 30° North and 60° West, we were in completely calm waters with the sun shining from a cloudless sky. One can understand why this place would be perfect to build a civilization on floating islands.

We stood on the deck just floating with our motors off. It was so calm and we felt like we were not moving at all. Such a serene place!

To think that deep down below us lay the sunken remnants of Atlantis. Sunk by its own hubris of moving too much stone onto floating islands. There is a certain irony to their doom, speaking to the tendency of rulers to build beyond their means.

Now it is all just spread across the ocean floor and their existence is just a cultural memory among the peoples that were drowned by the Atlantean sea people.

Our journey was now at an end in this tranquil place. The ocean around us lay motionless.

To my mind's eye, I could not help but envision this place as a gathering place for yachts that could meet up here like a modern-day sea people, simply to stay for a while in a sea so calm that they could remain here.

Yachts could then come and go, but if enough people did so, it could remain populated continuously. In such a way, a new floating Atlantis could be established in the Sargasso Sea, consisting of individual boats rather than islands. A real Polynavesia! A fitting way to commemorate the Lost Atlantis.

And it would have the benefit of not really needing a source of sustenance other than the willingness of the sailors to gather here.

With such musings, we took off from the site of Atlantis and went north to enter the North Atlantic gyre to go home the same way the Atlanteans must once have gone.